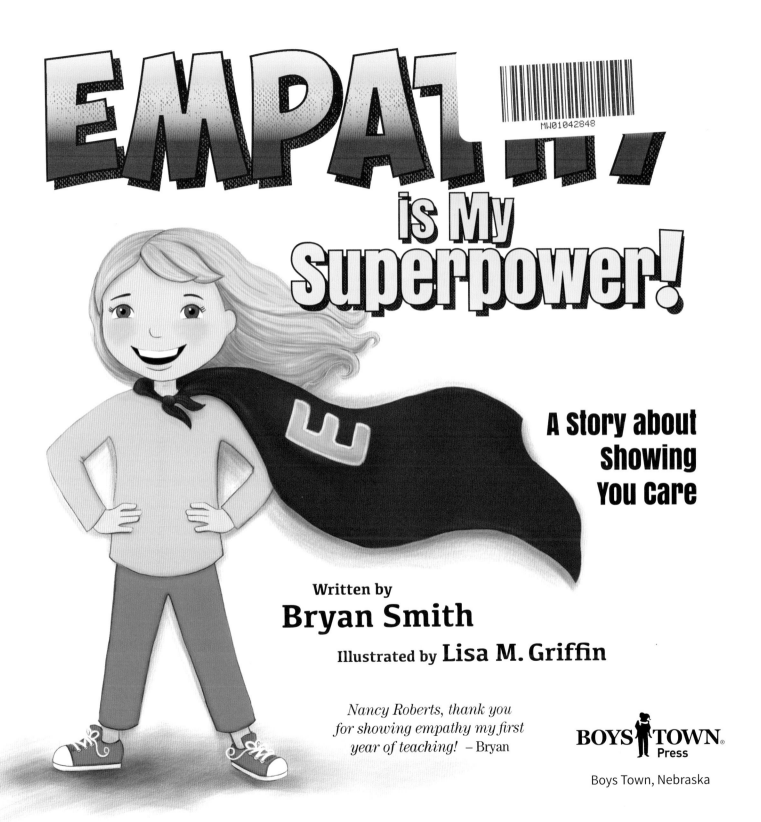

EMPATHY
is My
Superpower!

A Story about Showing You Care

Written by
Bryan Smith

Illustrated by **Lisa M. Griffin**

Nancy Roberts, thank you for showing empathy my first year of teaching! – Bryan

BOYS TOWN Press

Boys Town, Nebraska

Empathy is My Superpower!
Text and Illustrations Copyright © 2018 by Father Flanagan's Boys' Home
ISBN: 978-1-944882-29-7

Published by the Boys Town Press
13603 Flanagan Blvd.
Boys Town, NE 68010

All rights reserved under International and Pan-American Copyright Conventions. Unless otherwise noted, no part of this book may be reproduced, stored in a retrieval system, or transmitted in any form or by any means, electronic, mechanical, photocopying, recording or otherwise, without express written permission of the publisher, except for brief quotations or critical reviews.

For a Boys Town Press catalog, call **1-800-282-6657**
or visit our website: **BoysTownPress.org**

Publisher's Cataloging-in-Publication Data

Names: Smith, Bryan (Bryan Kyle), 1978- author. | Griffin, Lisa M., 1972- illustrator.

Title: Empathy is my superpower! : a story about showing you care / written by Bryan Smith ; illustrated by Lisa Griffin.

Description: Boys Town, NE : Boys Town Press, [2018] | Series: Without limits | Audience: grades K-6. | Summary: Amelia learns to be more understanding of others by imagining how they might feel in a challenging situation. If she can show she cares through her words and actions, she knows she has the power to improve relationships and help others. This is the third book in the Without Limits series.–Publisher.

Identifiers: ISBN: 978-1-944882-29-7

Subjects: LCSH: Empathy in children–Juvenile fiction. | Sympathy–Juvenile fiction. | Kindness–Juvenile fiction. | Friendship in children–Juvenile fiction. | Altruism in children–Juvenile fiction. | Helping behavior in children–Juvenile fiction. | Caring–Juvenile fiction. | Interpersonal relations in children–Juvenile fiction. | Children–Life skills guides. | CYAC: Empathy–Fiction. | Sympathy--Fiction. | Friendship–Fiction. | Kindness–Fiction. | Altruism– Fiction. | Helping behavior–Fiction. | Helpfulness–Fiction. | Caring–Fiction. | Interpersonal relations–Fiction. | Conduct of life. | BISAC: JUVENILE FICTION / Social Themes / Emotions & Feelings. | JUVENILE FICTION / Social Themes / Friendship. | SELF-HELP / Communication & Social Skills. | JUVENILE NONFICTION / Social Topics / Friendship. | EDUCATION / Counseling / General.

Classification: LCC: PZ7.1.S597 E46 2018 | DDC: [E]–dc23

Printed in the United States
10 9 8 7 6 5 4 3 2 1

Boys Town Press is the publishing division of Boys Town, a national organization serving children and families.

Hey everyone, Amelia here.

I'm a little tired right now.

Last night I was trying to get my beauty sleep (not that I need much!), when my **CRYBABY** brother started crying in his bedroom because his nightlight went out.

Why does he turn every little thing into the
BIGGEST problem in the world?

Boo-hoo, I say. Aren't we supposed to be teaching kids to toughen up?

Luckily, Mom came and replaced the lightbulb.
Then he **FINALLY** calmed down.

At breakfast, I "thanked" the **BIG BABY** for keeping me up half the night.

"But I was *scared* of the dark," he whined.

"Dude, you need to be **TOUGHER** than that. You're not two years old anymore."

"**STOP!**" Mom shouted. "Quit picking on your brother. You know, it wouldn't hurt you to show some empathy."

7

"Mom, I wasn't being mean. I was stating a fact. Kevin was acting like a baby. And besides, empathy isn't a REAL word."

"Amelia, you may think he was acting like a baby, but in his mind, he wasn't," Mom said. "Kevin really was scared. Don't you know what empathy means?"

"Not really," I said.

"It means you understand how others feel, and you give them support. It really isn't hard to show a little **EMPATHY.** Just follow these simple steps."

HOW TO SHOW EMPATHY

1. Think about how others may feel.

2. Come up with ways to show them you understand.

3. Offer any help or assistance you can.

"Let's try showing empathy now. How do you think Kevin felt when the nightlight went out?"

"Who knows? He probably thought some **HUGE MONSTER** was gonna come get him."

"He really might have. On a scale of one to five, how scared do you think he was?"

"probably a TEN, as loud as he cried!"

"Yes, he was really scared. That doesn't mean you would be scared in that situation. Different people handle situations differently. What could you do to show him you care?"

That's when I pictured myself as

"Be right back, Mom!"

11

I sprinted to my room, put my cape on, and then zoomed to the camping closet. Kevin always freaked out on camping trips when it got too dark, but he'd settle down and go to sleep if he had a flashlight. I tossed around all our camping gear until I found his favorite flashlight, and then I raced back to his room.

"Hey Kev, I'm gonna leave this by your bed in case the light goes out again. Just turn it on if you need some light."

A curious smile crossed his face. "Thanks, but **WHO ARE YOU?**"

"I'm **SUPER E!**, and the **E** stands for **EMPATHY.**"

"**What's that?**"

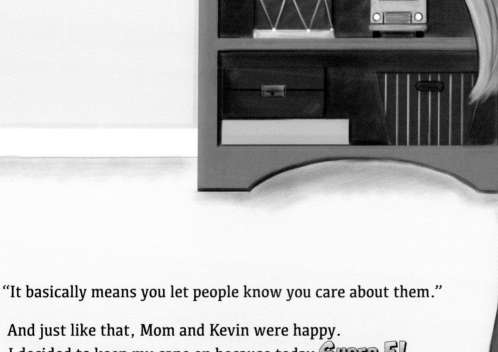

"It basically means you let people know you care about them."

And just like that, Mom and Kevin were happy.
I decided to keep my cape on because today **SUPER E!**
was going to spread caring and understanding at school.

13

As I walked the hallways, every kid looked at me like I was crazy.

14

Too bad they don't understand empathy. And it didn't take long before **SUPER E!** was called into action.

I had just sat down for lunch with my friends, like usual, when I saw Priya eating by herself—**AGAIN.** Priya always eats alone because no one wants to sit by someone who eats weird food all the time.

As I watched her, I remembered what Mom had told me about empathy. Then I asked myself how Priya must feel sitting all alone. I bet she's lonely eating by herself every day, and that can't be fun. **SUPER E!** needed to show Priya **EMPATHY.**

I sprung to my feet then quickly took a seat next to Priya. She didn't really look at me until I asked if I could eat lunch with her.

HOW TO SHOW EMPATHY

1. Think about how others may feel.

2. Come up with ways to show them you understand.

3. Offer any help or assistance you can

"Is this a joke or something? Why would you want to do that?"

"Because I don't like seeing you eat lunch by yourself, and I think you're cool," I said.

Priya smiled.

We started talking and had a good time. We actually had a lot in common, and I even found out the food she eats is made from recipes her grandparents brought from another country.

How awesome is that?

This **EMPATHY** thing is really powerful.

The next day in reading class, Kayla was really upset—**AGAIN.** She always says things like, "Why can't I learn like everyone else?" and "This doesn't makes sense!"

Her constant complaining was really annoying, so I shouted,
"Just try harder!" But then I remembered that whole empathy thing. Something really was bothering her, but what could I do to show her I cared?

I decided to get some advice from my favorite teacher, Mr. Parker. He asked if I knew exactly what was bothering Kayla. All I could say was that she was frustrated. Who knows why?

"Well, why not ask her yourself?" he said.

I marched over to Kayla and asked, **"What's wrong?"**

Kayla turned to me and said the words on the page didn't look right, and she needed help reading the questions.

"No problem," I said. "You just need your glasses. They must be around here somewhere."

"It's not that. My eyes are fine. It's something in my brain. I have dyslexia."

I learned people with dyslexia have a hard time reading words, and that's when I realized Kayla really had been trying her best the whole time.

With Mr. Parker's permission, I read the questions and answers to Kayla. She smiled and sighed with relief because everything made more sense. I told her I was sorry it was hard for her to read, and I'd help her anytime she needed it.

SUPER E! wasn't going to let someone struggle without offering to help.

Things at school were going great until I saw John in the hallway. I couldn't warn him in time, and he stepped in a puddle by the water fountains. His feet flew in the air, and he fell with a thud. Everything crammed in his backpack scattered across the floor.

Kids started laughing, and John was totally embarrassed. It was time for **SUPER E!**

"Have no fear, **SUPER E!** is here!"

I did a big ol' belly flop into the puddle and shouted, **"WOW! That's refreshing!"**

The hallway erupted in laughter as everyone pointed at me instead of John. We both got up, and then I helped him stuff everything back in his backpack. I even wiped up the floor.

"Why did you do that?" John asked. "Now you're soaking wet."

"Because 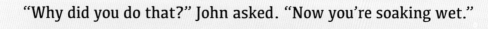 **SUPER E!** is all about empathy," I said.
"I care about you and wanted to help you out."

**Another person
saved by
SUPER E!**

25

The next day, my stomach hurt really bad. Without warning, I threw up right in the middle of Mr. Parker's spelling lesson. G-R-O-S-S! Eventually the nurse arrived with news that two **SUPERHEROES** had come to take me home.

Totally confused, I asked, "Two, who?" Just then Mom and Dad came around the corner. They were wearing capes, just like mine.

"Uh, what are you doing?"

"We're **MOM E** and **DAD E,** the superhero parents of **SUPER E!** We know feeling sick is awful, and we came here to show you how much we care."

They had a BIG surprise waiting for me at home.

28

They had made a **cozy nest of blankets** for me on the couch. There was a glass of soda and a box of crackers, too, in case I got hungry. Best of all, my favorite movie was ready to play on the TV!

CRACKERS

29

Even **SUPERHEROES** like me — **SUPER E!** — can benefit from a little **EMPATHY.**

Describing what kindness looks like can be difficult, but most agree it centers around how a child interacts with peers and reacts to the needs of others. Kind children have a high tendency to demonstrate **EMPATHY** toward their peers, siblings, and others in their lives.

Use the tips below to promote the development of empathy in children and to encourage a culture of kindness at home and at school:

1. **Reinforce that children (and adults) should treat everyone the way they want to be treated.** This can be especially difficult if someone perceives that another person is not treating him or her kindly. In these cases, it may be appropriate to remind children that two wrongs don't make a right, and help them see the value in taking the high road.

2. **Ask questions.** If you see someone experiencing a strong emotion, ask children how they think that person is feeling. See if they can identify the emotion and if there is anything they could do to help.

3. **Be a role model.** One of the best ways to teach empathy is to show empathy. Help children when they are struggling or hurt. Listen to them and show them you care.

4. **Help children descriptively label all of the emotions they are experiencing.** This can help them understand and show empathy to others who may be experiencing similar emotions.

5. **Have children take care of a pet.** Meeting the needs of a pet is a great way to help a child understand empathy. If housing or other arrangements preclude pet ownership, consider a fruit or vegetable plant that they can care for and nurture. Seeing the produce that results from proper handling of the plant will be enlightening.

6. **Perform random acts of kindness with your children.** Be sure to ask how it makes them feel, and ask them to speculate how the recipients of random acts of kindness feel.

For more tips on creating a culture of kindness, see *Kindness Counts* by Bryan Smith.

For more parenting information, visit boystown.org/parenting.

Saving Children   Healing Families

Boys Town Press books by Bryan Smith

Kid-friendly books for teaching social skills

Executive FUNction

978-1-944882-04-4

Downloadable Activities
Go to BoysTownPress.org
to download.

978-1-944882-11-2

OTHER TITLE: *What Were You Thinking?*

978-1-944882-20-4

978-1-944882-31-0

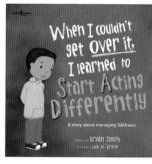

978-1-944882-22-8

978-1-934490-74-7

Without Limits — dream · connect · soar

Downloadable Activities
Go to BoysTownPress.org
to download.

978-1-944882-29-7

978-1-944882-12-9

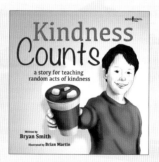

978-1-944882-01-3

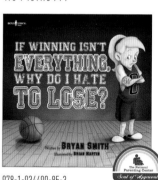

978-1-934490-85-3

BOYS TOWN® Press

**For information on Boys Town and its Education Model,
Common Sense Parenting®, and training programs:**
boystowntraining.org | boystown.org/parenting
training@BoysTown.org | 1-800-545-5771

**For parenting and educational
books and other resources:**
BoysTownPress.org
btpress@BoysTown.org | 1-800-282-6657